OSCAR

D. L. Smith

PAGE PUBLISHING, INC.
New York, NY

First originally published by Page Publishing, Inc. 2014

ISBN 978-1-63417-065-9 (pbk)
ISBN 978-1-63417-066-6 (digital)

Printed in the United States of America

Chapter 1

Born

I am new to the world. My mother cleaned me off with her tongue. Then she moved me up to feed on her belly. I drifted in and out of sleep when suddenly I could feel my sister, my brand-new sister, snuggle up next to me. I could not see yet as much as my eyes were not open, but I could sense a strong vision of light. I ate and slept and ate and slept then another birth. I felt my brother nudging his head against mine across me on my mother's belly. Oh, wow, I have a brother and a sister. This birthing event was repeated twice more. So at the end, I had two brothers and two sisters. Well, I still could not see yet, so I could not tell if they were brothers or sisters. I could only imagine what it might be like, but at least there were five of us after the birthing event was over.

I am the firstborn. I am the oldest. What a responsibility I have. I must guide them and set a good example for them to follow. All of this was going through my mind as I drifted off to sleep. I am feeling content with a belly full of mother's warm milk.

All of a sudden, this loud booming voice woke me as this big man came into the room. "Did that b——tch dog have a litter? I'll take care of them. I will bring them down to the creek and get rid of them. You told me you would keep her safe until we found the proper stud. If she has another litter, she will go down to the creek with her pups! I spent a lot of money to get you a full breed AKC Registered Collie. If we had the proper stud, these pups would be worth a lot of money. But no, you

3

let her run around outside with all the mutts and mongrels while she was in heat. No one must ever know she ever had this litter. We must keep her background and reputation clean. I'll take care of those pups once and for all."

I don't like to use that *B* word. Even though I know it means a female dog, it has another bad reflection on females in general. How could I think of this? I was just born. A puppy and I can't even keep my eyes open without falling back to sleep. Well, because the man sounded violent and determined, I could tell by the tone of his voice that word was not a good one. He scares me. How can I help save my family? What can I do? Maybe if I cry and yelp, it may wake my brothers and sisters and get them to cry and yelp. It would wake Mother. She has been so tired since she gave birth to us. But what could Mother do? Would I be putting her in more danger? God, I love my mother and would not want to place her in any danger. I drift into and out of sleep being feed by Mother's warm milk. I am not sure what days are, but I sense that my siblings and mine are over. But there is nothing I can do.

The man grabs a towel and then pulls us away from mother wrapping me, my brothers, and sisters in it. With all this commotion, mother wakes and has a sense of what is happening. She starts barking loudly and tries to bite the man.

Meanwhile, the little girl is crying. "Oh, Daddy, no, please let me keep them. I'll take care of them all."

The man says, "We can't afford the food they would need to eat. Besides, if anyone knows she had a litter from a common mutt, her breeding value will become nothing. I have a lot of money invested in that collie. I hope to breed her in the future. No one must ever know of this bad litter."

The man picked up the towel and left the house. Suddenly, I was very cold. I was freezing. I never experienced cold before, but I knew I did not like it. I missed the warmth of my mother's body. I could sense that it must be morning because I could hear birds starting to sing, along with their baby chicks peeping. I thought, "Why are they so happy?" I was jealous, but just moments before, I was just as happy. Then I realized I should be grateful for the little time I had, however short it may have been. After all, not all the eggs birds lay hatch. At least I had a day with my brothers and sisters, being alive and nurtured by our mother.

I could hear sharp crunching sounds as the man walked through the snow that had a thin layer of ice on the top. He was mumbling, "The creek is so low in winter that I must walk twice as far to reach the creek than it might take me to reach in the spring. While in summer, it could be totally dry. I think I could drop the pups here, and they would never survive without their mother. But maybe they could be found dead and traced back to my dog. No, even though it was snowing hard, almost blizzard conditions, I must walk another half mile through the woods to the creek. Then I will know for sure these pups will not come back to haunt me."

My sisters and brothers suddenly woke up and they started crying and whimpering. They knew something was wrong. Where is Mother? What is going on? They had no idea. What should I tell them? I decided it would be best not to say anything.

"Be quiet, pups. It will all be over soon." The man spoke softly as he shook the towel. Suddenly, I was falling from the towel. I landed in a snowdrift. I was surrounded by snow. The man never noticed I was missing or seen me fall. I dared not make a sound for fear the man would notice I was missing. I heard a splash. I heard the man say, "The cost of a towel is a lot less than it would cost me to feed those mutts. Worthless pups. Not breeding quality at all. I hope no one ever learns about these mongrels my show dog had given birth to."

I may freeze to death here. I might have been better if I was drowned with my brothers and sisters. I wonder if they ever noticed that I was not with them. I hope they don't think I abandoned them purposely. I hope somehow they all escape, but without Mother, how can we survive? Maybe Mother will somehow escape and rescue us. Although I know deep down that a rescue was impossible.

I heard the man walking back toward the house, the snow and ice crunching below his big feet. When the man arrives home, the little girl is holding the motherless dog crying. She is telling the dog, "I am so sorry for you to lose your babies so soon after giving birth to them."

The man says, "Stop that crying and carrying on. Those pups are worthless to us. In a few months, when she is in heat again, we will have her properly bred. Tomorrow I will have a six-foot chain link fence constructed around her shed in the back yard. That should keep any other mutts away from her."

The little girl replies, "Oh, Daddy, I just wanted a pet, not a money machine." The little girl is still crying.

Chapter 2

Rescued

A half a mile away and a few hours later, a school was letting out for the day. Steven and Debbie went to a combination elementary and junior high school, so they took the same school bus every day.

On this day, Steven told Debbie, "I must ask my science teacher about the upcoming science fair and about my project. Wait for me by the bus stop. If it takes a long time, we can always take the later bus home."

Debbie thought, "I am old enough to take the bus myself. If I wait till the late bus with Steven, it will be dark, and I won't have any playtime." Debbie gets on the bus and starts to look around. She suddenly realizes that these people are not the same ones from her regular bus. Then one of her classmates tells her, "Debbie, I think you are on the wrong bus because we don't live close to each other."

Debbie gets off the bus before it leaves the schoolyard. She is thinking, "I can walk home from here, but it is shorter if I cut through the woods instead of following the streets."

After a long night almost freezing to death, I was awake. It is midafternoon by now, and the sun has started to melt some of the snow around me. The ground below me has turned to mud, and I am covered with it. I am able to drink a little water, but it is not like mother's milk. It is cold and flavorless.

Suddenly, I can hear a little girl's voice singing, "Baa baa black sheep, have you any wool? Yes, sir, yes, sir, three bags full. One is for my master. One is, for the…" The singing stops as quickly as it started. The girl's boot comes down next to me, almost on top of me. The girl shouts, "My boot is stuck. I hope this is not quick sand like I saw in that movie last night. What is this? It's a little puppy. It must be freezing out here. I will put it in my pocket and take it home with me."

The girl reaches down and picks me up then puts me in her pocket. It is dark in here, but it is warmer than the snowbank. Debbie removes her boot and shoe that are stuck in the mud and then continues walking toward her home. She is walking awkwardly with only one boot on and the other foot only with a sock. She stops and sits on a large rock and removes her other boot and shoe. She leaves the other boot and shoe on the large rock. Debbie continues walking home in her stocking feet all wet and muddy.

Debbie enters the house and shouts, "Look what I found."

David sees Debbie without her boots or shoes covered with mud from her feet to her knees.

"Debbie, where are your boots and shoes? Look at you all covered in mud. Where have you been? Where's your brother Steven? He was going to take you home on the bus," David replied.

Debbie said, "David, look at what I found."

David replied, "I don't care what you found. Go to the bathroom and clean up."

David was the babysitter for Marcia's three children. She worked second shift. Sometimes, she would go out after work and not be home until very late.

"David, I found this little puppy in the woods next to where I lost one boot in the quick sand. I could not walk straight, so I left the other boot at the big rock."

David replied, "Well, Debbie, you better get yourself cleaned up. When Steven gets home, I will ask him to find your boots and shoes. You better go clean up now."

Suddenly, the front door burst open. Steven was standing there and started to shout, "David, you better call the police. Debbie is missing! I told her to wait for me by the bus because I had to ask my science teacher about doing research for the science project. You know, for the science fair. I told her I would only be a couple of minutes but to wait for me because we could always take the later bus together. The science teacher had to leave school early today, so I could not see her. When I got back to the bus zone, Debbie was not waiting there or on the bus. I described to the driver that she was six years old wearing a yellow dress and bright red boots. The bus driver told me he saw a girl matching that description getting on another bus. He did not know which bus it was or where it was going. We must call the police or the bus company. Mother will never forgive me for losing Debbie!"

"Steven, calm down. Debbie is in her bedroom crying. She came home missing her boots. I was concerned because she came home alone with no boots or shoes and with muddy socks."

"She may have thought I was mad more than I was concerned. You know how little girls can be. By the way, where is your other sister Susan?"

Steven replied, "Susan has dance class today. The instructor, Mrs. Molly, will drive her home around 5:30 PM."

"Steven, go talk to your sister. Calm her down please. Ask her to tell us her secret, and maybe we can find her boots before your mother finds out about her losing her shoes and boots."

Steven said, "Mother will blame me. She told me you're eleven years old and the one responsible to watch out for your younger sisters, who are eight and six years old."

Steven said, "My mother told me I am the man of the house while you are the guardian. You started taking care of us when Debbie was still in diapers. You are fifteen years old."

"Well, Steven, you're a little off. I am sixteen, not fifteen, but your mother will blame me before she blames you. Debbie was a lot easier to manage when she was in diapers than she is now! We should try to find her boots before your mother finds out they are lost. And where has she been while she was missing?"

While Steven and David were talking in the living room, Debbie managed to sneak into the kitchen and grab a little chunk of hamburger that was going to be used to make the meatloaf for dinner. Debbie took the raw meat to the little dog she hid in her dresser draw.

I could not still eat solid food since I only had mother's milk before. Debbie kept saying, "Come on, puppy, you must eat." Then she realized I could not eat solid food. I can only digest milk.

Steven called, "Debbie, I am home. I was scared you were lost. Please come here and show us your surprise that you told David about. He is not mad only worried that you came home alone without any boots or shoes."

Debbie entered the room carrying the puppy. "I found a puppy, but I think he's sick because he won't eat. Not even hamburger. Every dog eats hamburger."

David answered, "Debbie, it's a newborn. I would say less than three days old. New born puppies can only digest mother's milk for about four weeks before they can eat food."

Steven asked, "Where did you find him? If you found it outside, then someone tried to kill him. His mother would never abandon him or the other puppies that were born with him."

"What other puppies? He was the only one I found in the snow down by the creek."

"Debbie is that where you lost your boots?" David asked.

"Well yes," Debbie answered. "Well, one anyway. The other one is at the big rock after the creek."

Steven said, "I know where that is at. I will go down there and look for her boots if it is OK with you, David?"

"Yes, Steven, but you better take a flashlight. It may get dark soon, and I don't want to lose you," David answered.

Chapter 3

Cleaned

"Debbie, you get a medium-sized bowl and a dish towel. I will get some warm water. We don't want hot water or soap. It may bother his eyes or skin. We should get this dry mud off of this little dog. He is a mess," David said softly while trying to comfort her.

David thought, "It must have been a traumatic experience for Debbie today."

The front door opened again, and Susan claimed, "I am home. Where is everyone?"

"We are in the living room washing my new puppy," Debbie shouted.

At the same time, Steven entered through the back door. The house was built somewhat backward. The kitchen door faced the driveway and the road. The door into the living room faced the woods and swamps behind.

Steven announced, "I found her red boots and black shoes. One was at the big rock, and the other was about ten feet back toward the swamp. Debbie, what were you doing out there?"

"I missed the bus, and I thought it would be shorter to cut through the woods than walk along the streets," Debbie answered.

Susan interrupted, "So where did this puppy come from?"

David and Steven answered at the same time, "Debbie found him in the woods on her way home."

Debbie was getting excited and started to shout, "Steven, Steven, did you find his mother or the other puppies? Are they just outside?"

"Sorry, Deb, I could not find any of them," Steve said. "But I did look for them until it started to get dark." Steven did come across the other dead puppies, but he did not have the heart to tell Debbie.

"Must this puppy die because his mother can't feed him? I tried to give him hamburger meat, but he would not eat it." Debbie started crying. "Puppy, I told you I would save you, but I don't know how. I am so sorry!"

Susan told Debbie, "Don't worry. We can save him. I saw a movie in school how they save animals at the zoo without mothers. We must get some milk and something he can eat it from. I will get the eyedropper from the medicine cabinet, that should do for now. Tomorrow we will get some little baby bottles. Don't worry about this, Deb. We will raise this pup to be a champion!"

"What about our supper? I am getting hungry. Did you forget to cook for us with all this commotion?" Steven asks.

"Well, yes I did, but you can help me. I think you are old enough to learn. Do you want to learn how to make meatloaf?" David replied.

"Oh yes," Steve answered, "Anything so we can eat before the *Odd Couple* show comes on. You know Mother never lets us watch TV while eating."

Today has been a strange day. I think we can watch the TV and ignore that rule this one time. But we should have enough time to eat and do the dishes before the show starts. I also don't think your mother has to know about Debbie's little excursion. Just tell her that Debbie found the little dog, and we all want to keep it. I will talk to your sisters after we eat. I will peel and cook the potatoes. I will mix the meat with eggs and bread crumbs. You slice the mushrooms and onions. Then I will show you how to sauté them."

Steven was very happy to help until he started cutting the onions. He never cut onions before and did not know they made you cry. Steven said, "I don't know why I am so sad that my eyes are crying. I want that little dog to live."

"Steven, cutting onions makes everybody cry. Now start to cook them in this pan with a little butter and oil. You watch them, and as soon as they start to turn clear, then add a little more butter and add the mushrooms. It looks like everything is ready to go. Steven, you put this mix in the meatloaf. It should not take that long to cook. I will finish the vegetables."

Thirty minutes later, David announces, "Dinner is ready, let's all eat. We should be finished by the time the *Odd Couple* starts."

I am a warm puppy. Susan wrapped a hot water bottle in a towel and placed it under me on the sofa. Debbie kept trying to shove the warm milk into me until I could not drink any more. Warm and full, I fall into a deep sleep. I will never see my brothers and sisters. But now I have a new family of people who will want to love and care for me.

Chapter 4

Named

Steven asked, "Did everyone like the meatloaf I made?"

Susan replied, "I would have not eaten it if I knew you made it. I was sure David made it. It tasted like the meatloaf he always cooks. How did you know how to do it?"

"Well, David told me how to make it. I cooked the onions and mushrooms then added them to the meat, eggs and bread crumbs. Then I baked it in the oven. David cooked the other vegetables," Steve declared feeling proud of himself.

Susan shouted, "I don't care who taught you how to make it. Debbie and I would not have eaten it if we knew you made it."

Debbie screamed, "Don't include me, Susan. I liked the meatloaf. In fact, I want a meatloaf sandwich for my school lunch tomorrow."

Steven said, "Thank you, Debbie. I will make lunch for you tomorrow. Would you like mustard or mayonnaise on it?"

Debbie answered, "I want ketchup."

Susan still agitated replied, "Ketchup? How childish can you be?"

"No more bickering. Let's get to the dishes so we can all watch TV. The *Odd Couple* show doesn't start for another half hour. We should get the dishes done by then," David added.

After they all ate supper, Susan washed the dishes. Debbie dried them and Steven put them away.

Debbie inquired, "Why do I always have to dry the dishes? I always have to dry. Why can't I wash them or put them away?"

David replied, "Well, you are the smallest one. You can only reach the strainer. Steven and Susan can reach much higher to put the dishes away. That is the reason they swap between washing and putting them away. When you get bigger, you will be able to swap as well."

When the dishes are all put away, the four of them enter the living room and turn on the TV. Steven and David sit in chairs. Debbie and Susan sit on the couch, one of them on each side of me. I awoke, startled and still not sure of where I am. I am not hungry and warm. I feel much better than I did lying in a snowdrift by the creek and swamp. I do still miss my mother and sisters and brothers. I can't dwell on them. If I want to survive, then I must concentrate on myself. The man only wanted to kill us puppies and not my mother. I will find her someday. We will know each other by our scent. I will never forget mother's smell. Or will she mine. That is one thing that dogs have over people is a sense of smell.

Debbie said, "I still don't have a name for him. We can't call him puppy forever. He needs a name, not just any name but a real good one."

Steven and Susan both spoke, "We want to help you pick a name. After all, we don't want a dog with a stupid name."

An advertisement for the Academy Awards comes on the TV. "*Benji*, the movie about that little lost dog, is the favorite for the best picture Oscar. There are many other movies nominated for Oscars, so don't miss the awards Sunday night."

Debbie says, "That's it! I will name him Benji. If Benji is a famous name, I want my dog to have a famous name."

Susan tells Debbie, "You can't name him BENJI. Everyone knows what that famous dog looks like and it is nothing like your puppy. Your puppy looks more like Lassie than Benji."

"OK, Lassie will be his name," Debbie answered.

Steven protested, "Debbie, you cannot name him Lassie. Lassie means girl dog. You wouldn't like your name to be little boy, when you are a girl. He could develop a complex if you name him Lassie."

Debbie is a little frustrated and confused, when she asks, "What are the names of other famous male dogs?"

Everyone starts shouting out names, "Snoopy, Red Tin Tin, Old Yeller, and the Littlest Hobo. But he does not look like any of them."

I am the dog lying here between Debbie and Susan on the couch. I don't like any of these names for me. But I can't pick my own name. No dog or person has a choice in their name. It is given to them without a choice. Although some people have alias names or change them.

Debbie asks, "Well what makes these dogs famous?"

David replies, "They all had movies nominated for Oscars."

Debbie questions, "What is an Oscar anyway?"

Steven shouts, "Oh, I know. It's a prize for being the best. There is one for best movie, one for best actor and one for best actress. But I don't know if there has ever been one for best dog."

David says, "I don't think animals can win Oscars, only movies and people can. I think there might be another award for animals, but I don't know what it is called. Anyhow, the *Odd Couple* is about to start. We should all watch it together."

Felix, a photographer, has been out of town on assignment on the West Coast for a photo shoot for seven days. He arrives home and finds his roommate Oscar, a sports writer, has the place in a shamble. There are empty pizza boxes and empty Chinese food containers spread around the living room. Felix starts his allergy honking, "*Honk*, I can't believe what you have done to this place! *Honk*. What a mess you made of our place in only a week."

From the living room, Oscar shouts, "As long as you are in the kitchen, please bring me another beer from the Frig." Felix sees every counter space is covered with dirty dishes and silverware. The sink is piled halfway to the ceiling with dirty pots and pans.

Felix storms into the living room shouting at Oscar, "I am out of here. I am staying at a hotel until you have this place cleaned! I don't care how much it may cost you to hire someone to clean this place."

Mary, the police officer who lives below Oscar and Felix, bursts through the door. "What is all the shouting in here? I thought someone was being killed in here? Oscar, just looks at this place you made such a mess."

The milk Debbie fed me earlier was much richer than mother's milk. My system is not used to digesting it. I get cramps then I got the runs.

Debbie shouts, "Oh my god. Look at Oscar, he pooped all over himself and everything else."

Susan said, "You called him Oscar. Why?"

Debbie answered, "Well, that will be his name and that is final. No more TV or movie dog names. He is Oscar. But now I must clean him all over again. Why did he poop so badly?"

"Well, Debbie, he is not used to cow's milk. It is most likely richer than his mother's milk. You clean him again and I will line a box with a plastic trash bag and newspapers. In case he goes to the bathroom again, it will be in the box," Susan replied.

Debbie says, "Cow's milk? I gave him people's milk from the fridge and I even warmed it. He won't eat real food. What can we feed him?"

Steven tried to explain to Debbie, "People's milk comes from cows. I thought they would have taught that in school by now. Maybe we should get skin milk for Oscar. It doesn't have all the fat as regular milk."

"Maybe we should use baby formula. It might be better. I will ask your mother what she thinks when she gets home. Of course, I will have to explain to her why we all want to adopt this little puppy that he needs special care," David answered.

I now have a name. Oscar. Not what I would pick, but it is much better than puppy. I don't know what I would pick for a name, Oscar can mean best in one case and messy in another. I am sure I can like that name.

Chapter 5

Nursing and Training

The next morning, the children's mother, Marcia, was making breakfast and listened to the events of the day before. After all the versions of the story were told, Marcia suggested, "Maybe the puppy would do better having baby formula instead of cow's milk. I will give David money and ask him to go to the store to buy some bottles and baby formula for the puppy."

Debbie replied, "Mom, I did not give the puppy cow's milk. I gave him people milk from the refrigerator. His name is Oscar. Please don't call him the puppy. But how long must he eat only milk, and not dog food?"

Susan said, "I have library class today. I will look for a book on how to grow puppies and train them. That should tell us how to do it right."

Steven jumped up from the breakfast table and shouted, "I called my friend last night. He told me that the vet said you can use canned milk, egg yolks, vitamin drops, and something else, it may be yogurt, to make a healthy puppy formula."

Marcia said, "We will try baby formula first, and if it still makes the puppy sick, I will call the vet myself and see what he has to say. Now you must all get ready for school. Debbie, if you miss the bus, do not leave by yourself. I don't want you cutting through the woods. Steven, you make sure Debbie is on the same bus as you from now on."

Both Steven and Debbie replied, "OK, Mother," both knowing it was lip service that may not be true because they were both independent, not wanting their mother to know the truth. Steven has his friends, and he does not like his little sister tagging along. Debbie does not want to be controlled by her older brother. She finally now has some independence, however little it may be.

Susan adds her opinion, "Oh, Mother, you know as well as anybody else that is never going to happen. If I can take control of Debbie, I'll make sure she does what I tell her!"

"No, no," Debbie protested. "Stevie and I will be OK together. I don't want Susan telling me what to do. She always treats me like I am still a baby and I can't try anything I want to do."

Steven hated to be called Stevie, but he could tolerate it from Debbie. When he was in the first grade, his mother called him Stevie, and the whole class picked up on it and called him, "Stevie is a weakling" until the fourth grade. He hated it, and in the fifth grade, he got into a fistfight about it. He declared, "No one will call me Stevie unless they want *a face full of my fist.*"

They used to say, "Stevie is a baby name." But Debbie was his baby sister. He kept asking her to call him Steve or Steven. Again he said, "Debbie, did I asked you not to call me Stevie?"

"OK enough. You must all hurry off or you will be late for school. I will call David and tell him to get the stuff for the puppy before he gets here today," Marcia replied.

"Oscar is your name, Oscar is your name," Debbie kept telling me that while she feed me more warm milk from the eyedropper before she left for school. I was left alone for hours while the children went to school and Marcia went to work.

David gets out of school about one hour before the children do. He went to Jack King's store and bought baby formula and Playtex disposable bottles. When he arrived at Marcia's house, the children were just arriving in the school bus.

Debbie rushed in shouting, "David, did you get the food for Oscar? He must be starving by now. I have been at school all day and I could not feed him."

"Debbie, don't worry. Your mother left me a note telling me she fed him just before she left for work. But you better clean his box again before you try to feed him," David answered.

Susan enters proclaiming, "I went to the library and found a book on how to raise puppies. It has a chapter about if the mother dies or abandons her puppies."

Steven asked, "Why would a mother dog abandon her puppies?"

"If a person or other animal touches the newborn before the mother cleans them off, then the mother smells the other scent and not her own. She will think some other animal is trying to take over," Susan answered.

Debbie asks, "Oscar has been without his mother for a while. He is still alive but won't eat puppy food. How long must I keep feeding him the bottle? Does your book tell you that, Susan?"

"The book says four to five weeks for the mother to nurse a puppy, but if the puppy observes the mother eating regular dog food, it may start on solid food earlier."

Debbie turned to David and said, "Here is my allowance money. I want you to buy dry puppy food and a big box of Cheerios. I will mix them together in Oscar's bowl. I will eat the oats but pretend that I am eating the puppy food. After all I am the closest thing Oscar has to a mother." David replied, "Debbie, you will be the best trainer in the world for the puppy. No, I must call him Oscar. If it was not for you, he would have died out there all alone. But you keep your money."

Three weeks later, Oscar is eating solid food. A week before the puppy training book described. Debbie religiously changed his box several times a day, but now Oscar is bigger and getting out of his box. Sometimes leaving messes in unexpected places.

Debbie asked David, "After school tomorrow, can you take me to the public library to get a book on how to house train a puppy? I don't want Susan to get it because she will act bossy about it. I want to do this myself."

"Debbie, you don't have a library card, but it's about time you get one. If they don't give you one, I will put the book on my card. They should give you on as long as you can sign your name. You should be old enough to have one."

The next day, David and Debbie went to the public library. Debbie had no problem getting a library card. She checked out a book about how to housebreak and train your dog or a book with a very similar title.

Debbie proudly presented the book to her brother and sister saying, "Look at this book I got at the library today."

Susan said, "That book is from the public library. David must have checked it out for you because even I don't have a library card from the public library!"

"Well, I have one," Debbie replied, swiftly pulling the card from her pocket and waving it in front of Susan.

Susan, jealous and upset, said, "Well, I will go down there tomorrow and get one myself. If they will give you one, they will have to give me one!"

David told Susan, "You can't go there by yourself. Ask your brother Steven if he will take you. In order to get a card, you must be there with someone with a card to verify who you are. I cannot go with you tomorrow because I have baseball practice after school."

Steven said, "Susan, I will take you. I know how I would feel if you got your card before I got mine."

"Susan, will you help me read this book? Some of the words are too big for me to understand by myself," Debbie asked, realizing she upset Susan and was trying to make amends. "David and Steven will make supper and we can go into the living room while they cook," she added. Susan and Debbie left the room and turned on the TV.

Steven asked David, "What are we cooking for supper? I am glad you are teaching me how to cook."

"Beef and macaroni, well, that is what I call it. It is macaroni, beef, onions, peppers, and mushrooms with crushed tomatoes and stewed tomatoes. First cook the macaroni. Then you sauté onions, pepper, and mushroom. After that, fry the hamburger and put it all in a big pot with the tomatoes and simmer, stirring until warm. Serve with grated cheese and bread with butter."

Debbie and Susan are in the other room exploring various methods of house breaking a puppy or dog. The book suggests that it is easier to do while it is still a puppy and not when it becomes a dog because bad habits are harder to break the longer they are part of every-day usage. It is like when a person tries the first cigarette. They are not addicted, but after a couple of packs, they cannot stop. It can become a lifelong bad habit.

Debbie said, "I don't want to keep Oscar in a closet, and we don't have a big crate to lock him into."

Susan said, "Mother will not allow us to just let him run around and poop all over the house. We must find another way to train Oscar."

"I know how," Debbie shouted. "My old play pen is still in the basement. I will ask Steven or David to bring that up. There is some leftover carpet down there also. I will ask him to cut a piece half the size of the pen. I want some small rocks, some sand, and regular dirt."

Susan said, "You can't leave Oscar in the pen all the time. It will make the whole house stink even after you make the changes required every day. The book said between fifteen and twenty minutes after eat-ing, the puppy usually has to go. You have to take him outside to where you want him to go. If he does go, you should give him a treat and say, *good dog, good boy,* or *good Oscar.* But you must reward him for going outside and not in his little room. Once he starts going outside, you should let him out of the playpen. If he has an accident in the house, take him back outside to where he should go. If he keeps pooping in the house, then you place him back in the pen. Sooner or later, he will get the idea where he should go outside."

Steven brought up the old playpen and lined it with the carpet. However, David told them, "No rocks, sand, or dirt. Oscar must not confuse inside and outside where he can go potty. Oscar is a quick learner, and soon he will let everyone know when he wants to go out-side by barking and waving his tail by the door."

I quickly realized that I could do this any time I wanted to go out, even if I did not need to go to the bathroom.

It was Saturday morning. Marcia had a date the night before, so David stayed over. David always kept extra clothes at their house for such occasions.

Debbie assembled everyone in the living room and announced, "The book about dog training says to only feed the puppy twice a day. About fifteen to twenty minutes later, take it out to go to the bathroom. Always take it to the same place and wait for the puppy to go. When the dog goes, tell him *good dog* and give him a treat. If the dog leaves a mess that you don't discover until later, do not scold the dog because he won't understand. The dog will not relate to the earlier event with the current punishment. However, if you catch him in the act, you may say bad dog. Don't hit him or rub his nose in it. Just take him and the poop outside where he is allowed to go. Sooner or later, the dog will learn to let you know when it needs to go. Now, I will feed Oscar when I first get up in the morning. I will then take him out fifteen minutes later. I will wait for him to go before I come back in. I will then feed him again in the early evening. I will get up earlier every day to do this again before I go to school. No one else should feed him unless I ask you to. Understand?"

Debbie would take me outside early every morning after feeding me, then again later in the early evening. She would tether me by my leash to the tree. I could only move ten feet in any direction. Debbie would sit on her little swing and sing or recite nursery rhymes. "Baa, baa black sheep, have you any wool? Yes, sir, yes, sir, three bags full. One for my master, one for my dame, and one for the little boy that lives down the lane."

"Debbie, you must come in now or you will be late for school," Marcia shouted into the back yard.

"But Oscar did not go yet!" Debbie replied.

"Well, bring him in and try later after school. You can't miss school because of the puppy. It may take a long time to train a new puppy. You will have to be patient, but you must go to school."

Debbie replied, "OK, Mother, but I wish everyone would call him Oscar instead of that puppy."

I was placed back in my modified pen and slept for a little while. When I woke, I had to go. I did not want to mess my blanket or pillow. I made it out of my pen and walked to a small corner. When Debbie arrived home from school, she saw what I did. Instead of yelling at me, she took a small sand shovel, scooped up my mess and placed it a small pail. Debbie then put me on the leash and tied me to the tree and emptied the bucket in that area.

"Oscar, this is where you should go. Not in the house. Now let's go back in. It's time to feed you and try again later," she whispered into my ear softly not trying to upset me.

Susan who shares the bedroom with Debbie and Oscar's pen complained, "This room stinks. I don't think Debbie is doing it right. I would smack him and rub his nose in it. That is the way to housebreak a dog!"

Steven said, "I helped Debbie read that book she got from the library. That is another way to train a dog, but it teaches a dog by fear not by love. If you want the dog to be afraid of the owner, then that is the way to train it."

It was about six months after Debbie found Oscar when David announced, "Oscar has been going to the bathroom outside on a regular basis. I think it is time we take him out of the pen and let him roam the house. If he starts pooping around the house, we can always put him back in the pen."

Debbie replied, "Oh, David, I agree. He is getting too big to keep in the pen. Oscar is old enough now to behave OK in the house. We can put his food and water dish in the kitchen."

Oscar is delighted to be out of the pen, his personal prison. The people don't know that he has been getting in and out of this pen when there has been no one home or late at night when everyone is sleeping. At first, he runs through every room in the house, smelling everything. Soon this infatuation wears off.

Susan inquires, "Where will he sleep? I don't want him on my bed. How will he know where to sleep?"

Steven said, "I know. I will take his blanket and pillow out of the pen. Then place them where the pen is now. I will clean and wash the pen then put it back in the basement."

"Thank you, Steven. Good idea. I will wash his blanket and pillow case," Debbie replied.

"No, Debbie, don't wash them. We want him to smell himself on them. Not until he gets use to sleeping there. Maybe after a while you can wash them," David interjected.

Oscar loved his new freedom and was determined not to disappoint this family. His thoughts are, "I must try my hardest to prove to this family that I have overcome the loss of Mother's natural training, eating solid food, and becoming housebroken. Most puppies receive basic training from their mother. Debbie was a very good substitute as young as she was. Someone older would have had a lot less patience and understanding. I am now on the journey from being a little puppy to a large puppy and a small dog. I must always go to the door and bark when I need to go potty or relieve myself."

For a while, everyone in the house puts Oscar on his leash and takes him out when Oscar barked by the door. Debbie was the only person who would remove the leash once outside. She would then put it back on Oscar before coming in.

Often, when I did not have to go to the bathroom, each of the children would put me on the leash and walk me along the road. They would take me to the playground, the church, or a schoolyard. I liked the park the best. There were always other dogs at the park. I always hoped that one or more of my brothers or sisters were rescued like I was. I did not expect to see my mother because the man that tried to kill me was so mean. He would never let that little girl take my mother to a public place after I was born. Maybe I could run into my father but I would never know. He was not present when I was born, and we would not have the scent recognition like I would have with my siblings or my mother.

When Debbie took me out, she would remove my leash and let me run around by myself. Debbie whispered into my ear, "When I was two and three years old, my mother kept me in a harness. It is much like a leash and I hated it. So when I call you, you must come back. Otherwise, I will keep you on a leash."

Susan would take me to the park. She would walk me on my leash till we got there, then she would put me on some type of a device called a swing. She would tie me in it then push me into the sky. I did not like it at first, but after a little while, I found it exciting and thrilling. It was at this time that I realized that people of different ages are very different. I know this may sound confusing or stupid to the reader, but it was a revelation to a little dog like me. Yes, now I consider myself as a little dog, and I am Oscar, no longer a puppy.

Chapter 6

Little Dog

Steven takes me to a baseball field at the high school where David goes to. They let anyone play there. Steven is on a team and wears a uniform on the days he plays. Steven taught me the difference between a baseball and a tennis ball. The baseball is hard and made of leather. I should never chase or catch a baseball, especially if the boys are wearing uniforms. Tennis balls are soft, fuzzy, and chewable. Steven would toss the tennis ball and tell me to fetch. I loved this game. I could play for hours at a time. Usually, Steven would get tired of playing before I would. Every time we played hard like this, I would sleep a lot deeper and have nicer dreams. There are other balls I was exposed to. A softball is a lot like a baseball, hard and leathery, but it is a lot bigger. Basketballs, footballs, and beach balls are very strange. I once broke Debbie's beach ball by biting it. My favorite one is the tennis ball.

Debbie and Susan had friends that were mostly little girls. Debbie's friends were younger than Susan's. Sometimes, they had the same friend in both of their circles of friends. On more than one occasion, fights between Susan and Debbie broke out over which friend was whose. Sometimes, the friends would take sides, but more often than not, they would be diplomatic and claim to be friends of both.

Susan and Debbie both dressed me in people or doll's cloths. Susan would put ballerina dresses and other frivolous clothes on me. Debbie was more of a tomboy. She would dress me in short pants and tee shirts. I did not like either. I am a dog and I don't want to wear people clothes. When Steven or David seen them dress me up, they would tell the girls it was wrong and may affect or confuse my mental status as a young male dog.

David brought me a new toy called a Frisbee. It was a little flying saucer. Unlike a ball, it would fly up in the air where I could chase it. Then I would jump high into the air to catch it before it fell to the ground. It was a lot more fun than chasing a ball. The girls realized how much I liked it, so they all would take this new toy out when they went out to play with me.

It was about this time in my life when Debbie announced to everyone, "Oscar is old enough to be let out alone. He does not need anyone to take him to go the bathroom. If he wants to run around by himself, he should be able to. We do not live in a city that has a leash law. He should be allowed to be free. If he decides to run away, then that should be his decision. We can't keep babying him all his life. He's no longer a puppy. He is a little dog, and he should be treated like one. This also means no more dressing him in people clothes. I hope everyone understands this because if you don't, I will be all over your case."

Both David and Steven applauded Debbie for this little speech. David said, "Debbie, the puppy is not the only one growing up, but you are too. I am glad to watch you grow up. If it wasn't for you, Oscar never would have survived his first few weeks. Everyone must follow Debbie's directions about Oscar. Except when we take him somewhere when we must walk along the streets, we must keep him on his leash. I have observed that Oscar has a tendency to chase cars. That could be deadly for him. I once had a dog that kept chasing cars until he finally got hit and killed. I know how to train a dog to break this habit. Until I get this training done, only let him out close to home without his leash."

Well, I am both happy and disappointed. I can go out alone; but I still must be escorted to the park, the playground, and the church. I must first explore the woods where I was first found. However, I do not want to find the graves of my brothers and sisters. I will try to remember where I got dropped accidently and not go deeper into the swamp. Instead, I will try to trace back to where my mother was. If any of my brothers or sisters survived, I am sure they would try to trace back to our mother. If anyone would know, she would. I am walking out the back from the house into the woods.

Suddenly, instead of more woods, I am at a road. This road is not like the quiet road in front of the house where I live. It has a lot of cars, trucks, and busses speeding very fast. There is no way across. I can't try to cross this road without being killed. What have I done? The first time I go out on my own, I am in as much danger as I have ever been in. I have to go back to the woods and try to find my way home. By now, it is getting dark, and when I get into woods and trees, I am not sure these are the same clump of woods and trees that I left in the morning. I decide that since I do not know what way to go, I should just sleep until daylight. Then I could probably get a better sense or scent of direction. After all, I forgot that I peed on different trees on my way here. I just hope I can sleep.

Debbie, Susan, and Steven wake up and realize that Oscar never came home from the previous night. Steven and Debbie open both the front and back door calling out, "Oscar, Oscar, where are you?"

Marcia tells them, "You kids must get ready for school. I will call David and ask him to cut through the woods on his way here and to look for Oscar when he comes today."

Suddenly, Oscar is barking at the back door. I was not really lost. I was tired and confused. If I kept going instead of sleeping, I would have gotten lost. People don't understand what I think; at least, I don't think they do. Debbie kept me tied up for the next two days. She would put the leash on me to go out to the bathroom.

David told Debbie, "You can't keep punishing him by keeping him locked up. Otherwise, he will want to run away when he is free. Maybe he was chasing cars and got confused to where he was. I will start to train Oscar not to chase cars if you would like?"

"Yes, David that might be good," replied Debbie.

"Well, I know of a few methods to stop a puppy or dog from chasing cars, trucks, and motorcycles. However, everyone who takes Oscar out must follow the same training method. Otherwise, it will just confuse him and not break this bad habit. Not everyone always agrees on the best way to break this habit. Some people think a particular method may be cruel. That person may try to use a different way, thinking it is less cruel. But this will only confuse him and take him longer to break this bad habit. If he is not broken of this bad trait, it could eventually kill him. So before we start a training program, we must have a family conference. I will set it up for 11:00 AM on Saturday."

Saturday morning, everyone is there seated around the kitchen table. David reiterated what was said above for two reasons. The first reason was Marcia and Steven were not there when he first said this. The second reason was he really wanted Susan and Debbie to understand fully. "I will try to explain each option individually covering the pros and cons, followed by any questions anyone may have."

"After I described every method and answered any questions, everyone must agree on the best way to proceed." David continued, "The first method is one my grandfather told me about. You need to get a stick about four feet long and about two inches in diameter. Then you get a piece of rope like clothesline rope, long enough to swing the stick between his knees from his collar. The pro for this method is as the dog chases the vehicle, the stick will swing back and forth hurting his knees. You must only apply this when the dog chases something you think will endanger him. The pros and cons are almost the same for this method. When the dog start chasing something, the stick will swing and hit him in the knees inflicting some pain. Hopefully, it will break his habit from chasing whatever it is. On the other hand, if he just ignores the pain, he can hurt himself. Anyone have questions?"

Steven asked, "What if there is a lot of traffic and instead of the stick hitting him on the knees, it gets caught between his legs? Won't he fall in the middle of the street?"

"Good point, Steven. When my grandfather trained dogs, we only had a couple of cars a day come down the street. I think we should rule this method out," David answered.

Oscar did not understand the idea of options or of multiple methods. So immediately, his thoughts began, "Oh my god, if they try this on me, it may kill me. I am addicted to chasing things. It is bred into all dogs. Since we evolved from earliest dog incarnations, we had to chase to get food. It is an inbred habit that I cannot avoid."

"The next method is something I just read about. I am not sure it would work, but I will tell you about it anyway. This method uses water balloons. You fill a bunch of balloons with water and take them with you. As soon as Oscar starts to chase a car or truck, you hit him with a water balloon. The pro of this method is like having a bucket of water thrown on a dog for bad behavior. The con is if you miss the dog with the balloon, he will never realize the punishment. Anyone have questions?" David asked again.

Susan stood and said, "Oscar loves water and water balloons. Wouldn't this encourage him to chase cars and trucks even more?"

Marcia spoke up for the first time since she has been observing David began to hold this family conference, "I do not want my children throwing water balloons into the street. If they miss Oscar, they may hit the car behind him. God forbid someone with an open window gets hit with a water balloon thrown by one of my children. This option is absolutely out."

Oscar thought, "I like water balloons as much as I like chasing things. It is one splash of cool water as opposed to a hose that has water that is getting colder all the time. I hate hoses of water but love water balloons."

David starts again, "The third method is an electronic dog collar. This is a special collar you place on the dog. It has an electrical shock that although feels unpleasant; it does not permanently hurt or damage the dog. The dog walker has a small device with a button that when pressed gives the dog a small painful but not damaging shock around his or her neck. If the dog does not stop, you can increase the charge.

"The dog will not want to run anymore, so it will stop chasing the car or truck. When this happens, the dog will associate chasing cars or trucks with this unpleasant feeling. The pro of this method is it almost always works as long as the collar is used only to stop chasing cars. The con is the collar can only be used for one training method at a time and must be removed after the desired behavior is learned. It should remain off for at least three or four weeks before you use it again for another training purpose. Anyone have any questions?"

Debbie speaks up and says, "I don't like the idea of Oscar being shocked. Will it hurt him? He still is a small dog. I am not sure I like this method. Are there any other methods?"

"The last method that I know about is one of the automatic leashes. They let out a long line that lets the dog run until you push a button that stops and locks the line. As soon as the dog starts to chase the car, you lock the leash and pull back on it hard. This will stop the dog in his tracks. The pro is this method works well as long as it is consistently applied. The con is it could also cause the dog to fall. So you may not want to use this on a busy street," David replied.

Marcia said, "My concern is Oscar is growing bigger and faster than Debbie is. If she tries to lock the leash, he may pull her down and drag her into the street. I think the best method is the electric collar. I will go to the pet store later today and buy one. End of discussion, that is my decision."

"Well, the most important thing is whatever method is used, it must be constant. Not used once in a while but always. The smarter the dog, the faster it will learn. Oscar is a very smart dog, and it should not take long to train him," David responded.

"I don't think I like the idea of wearing an electric collar. But David thinks I am smart, and it won't take that long. I don't have much of a choice of what I wear, but at least it is not an electric dress," Oscar thought.

Chapter 7

Mother's Visit

I no longer chase cars or trucks. So now I am allowed out on my own again. One day after cutting through the woods, I think I recognize the house I was born in. I can see the little girl that tried to save me and my siblings. She is much older now. I guess everyone is, but you don't notice those things with people that you live with every day. It is starting to get dark so I will go back home and come back another day. I hope to find my mother here, so I will not forget the way. I do not want to become obsessed with my mother's home, but I will try to come back to see her in the future. My only hope is that she will still live here and that man has not treated her badly. Oscar walks back through the wood home getting home before anyone starts to worry about his whereabouts.

A year has gone by. Steven is too old for a babysitter, but he does not want to babysit or take care of his sisters. Besides, they would not listen to him anyway. David and Marcia have become good friends, and occasionally, Marcia asks David to sit for one of her friend's children along with Susan and Debbie. The children are younger and one is still in diapers, but David does not mind because he does get paid a little extra when the younger children stay over.

Oscar on the other hand has to show more tolerance. "These two boys, one four and the other not quite two, try to pull my ears and my tail. The older boy tries to put the young one on me to ride me like a horse. God, I hate this, but I can't retaliate. I do yelp but do not bark.

David will hear, and then yell at the boys. He will tell them that I am not a toy for them to play with. After one of these incidents, I feel the need to get out. One evening, I was out and watched David leaving to go home. I always wondered where David lived, so I followed him home. I kept far enough behind him, so he never knew I was following him. I was actually proud of my ability to do this stealthy thing. I was lying outside of David's back door when a dog from the house next door enters the yard and starts barking and growling at me. I am feeling defensive and growl and bark back. There is no way that I am going to let this aggressive dog get close to David's door."

The barking and growling gets very loud when David opens the door and shouts, "What is going on out here? Oscar, you should not be here. You must have followed me home. Fritz, it is OK, you go home now." Fritz left and went next door back to his home. "Oscar, you better get in here. I will take you home in the morning before I go to school. Oscar, you are a bad dog for following me."

Oscar was thinking, "I thought David would be happy to see me here, but I guess not. He will take me back, and the others will also be mad at me. I wish I could know better. How can I learn to do what is right?"

The next morning at Marcia's house, everyone is concerned that Oscar did not come home again staying out all night. Soon, David arrives with Oscar on a leash and explains what happened the previous night.

Debbie is upset and yells, "Oscar, when will you understand this is where you live? This is the place you should come home to every night. I am going to punish you by putting on the leash tied to the tree out back for days until you learn. If you do not learn from that, then I will take more drastic action."

At first, Oscar did not understand why he was locked to the tree. But every day someone from the family would come down and try to explain why he was being punished. What he should do in the future to avoid punishment. After a while, Oscar figured out that, "Even if I don't know what is wrong, if I act humble and loving I will be forgiven and released."

Oscar was correct in his thinking. After only a few days, he was allowed to roam free again. His first thoughts are, "I will not follow people, but I will look to see if I can find my mother. I think I remember the way to the house I visited a few weeks ago. Maybe she can give me advice on how people act and think."

Oscar was careful not to stay out or go far away during the night. After eating and watching the children go to school, he wandered into the woods. I do remember the way through the woods back to that girl's house. That's where my mother lived. When I arrived at the house, I do not see anything happening. I decide to walk around to the backyard. There I see a fenced in area with a chain-link fence. Inside I see a couple of puppies exiting from a large shed. They look like my sisters and brothers did the last time I'd seen them. I bark softly because I do not want to alert anyone to hear me except my mother.

Mother emerges from the shed or doghouse. She is happy to see me because she thought I had died along with my brothers and sisters. However, she warns me that I am putting my new brothers and sisters along with her in danger and at a high risk because I showed up there. She explained that most puppies once removed from their mother and siblings never get to see them again. She tells me that fathers almost never see their puppies, and I am old enough now to think about becoming a father. I left there, happy to see her again, but a little sad knowing I would never see her or any siblings again. I realized that I grew up a little and matured very much from this visit, but I will never visit again.

It is not quite dark when I arrive back from the woods, and I decide to pay a visit to that French poodle that lives three houses away from me. I think she has been flirting with me. After a short visit, I return home before it gets totally dark. I don't want to be yelled at or punished again.

I followed David to school, but I would sit outside just looking in the windows. One warm spring day, the big old windows to the classroom were open. I could see David inside, sitting at a small desk, but it looked like he was falling asleep sitting there. I thought David would rather play than be sitting there. I jumped through the open window and started to lick David all over his face. The whole classroom exploded in shouts and cheers.

The teacher shouts, "David, take your dog and report to the principal's office immediately." The man is yelling at David about not allowing the dog to come to school. He said, "You will be suspended for three days." I just thought David would be glad to see me.

David scolded me all the way home, "Oscar, you are a bad dog, you will be punished. I am going to tie you to that tree and keep you there until I can go back to school." When David told the others what I had done, they all agreed with my punishment.

Chapter 8

Moved

The company Marcia works for closes, and they move their factories to China. After a while of collecting unemployment, Marcia had to go on welfare as a result. She is very proud and determined person, with a positive attitude, so she does not allow this to depress her.

Marcia's ex-husband has not able to send the checks he is supposed to. He lives in another state with a new family, and he is struggling to make ends meet there. Marcia and her ex split up in a very friendly manner. They both realized it was time for them to part their ways. Neither of them wanted it to upset the children in a negative way. They both want the best for each other. The children are never in the middle of a dispute.

As a result, she can't keep up the payments on the house. She has to move to the federal housing projects. Marcia likes living the projects since there is no yard work or snow removal required. The children are not convinced yet. But it is nearer to school and the bus stop is closer. There are a lot more children who live in the projects than in their old neighborhood. There are more children around the same age as them, so it doesn't take long for them to prefer living in the projects.

The projects were built in the early 1950s. They consist of twelve brick buildings, each of which contains eight apartments, side by side, not on top of each other. There is a gap between the lower six buildings and upper six buildings. In between is a cross walk. The children and some of the young adults formed sports teams. The teams they called the "lower cross" and the "upper cross" teams. David, although he lived outside of the projects, lived below the crosswalk. He was allowed to join the lower cross team. Marcia and her children lived above it and belonged to the upper cross team. Often on the weekends, games between these teams took place in the large field behind the projects. The games played usually depended on the season. Sometimes, more often than not, fights or arguments would break out between them. One time David and Marcia's children did not talk for a week. They just passed written notes between themselves.

There were two more of these project complexes built in this city. Our city was considered a low-income and depressed area. The surrounding towns are very affluent and high-income communities that would never accept low-income projects without a highly financed fight. Thus three were built here.

These units are designated for low-income households, many with single mothers with children. Over the years, the projects acquired the nickname of "The Brick Jungle South, The Middle Brick Jungle, and Brick Jungle North." On occasion, disputes and outright fights would break out between them. During the late 1960s and early '80s, the projects were a haven for drug and theft activities, which contributed to the source of the fights. We lived in the Middle Brick Jungle. If a dispute developed between us and another project, the lower and upper cross gangs united. They became known as the "Cross Street Bullies."

The middle projects are located on the other side of the woods, behind the old house, so it is really not that far away. David lives in the house, on a street just outside of the projects, so he is a lot closer now.

I like living in the projects because there a lot more people and other dogs that I can visit. I no longer followed David to school. I am allowed to go to the elementary school and wait for recess, so I can play with the children. I must leave the school yard once the children go back into the school. As long as I only go there when the children are outside, I don't have any problems. I often lay hidden in the woods outside of the school, waiting for the children to come out. After school, all the children get on busses to go home. I know it is then time for me to get home.

I know the house my mother lives in is not that far away, but I don't know how to get there from here. I can find it from the woods. I will start from there, but I will not contact my mother because of my last visit. I will lie out of site. I would just like to see her once again. I am shocked when I get there. The house is in the process of being torn down, and there is a strip mall being put up behind the house. Well, now I know I will never see my mother again. Instead of going back through the woods, I can see the project just two blocks away along the road.

The family is getting older. I do not understand how time goes by or why people change when they get older. So some of the events that I describe next are most likely not in the order of when they happened. It's more like I recall in a random order. After all, I am just a dog.

Steven no longer wanted me going with him. He had new friends that did not want a dog to tag along. If I followed him, he would take me back home and put me in the house. Susan and Debbie are in junior high school. They take me along with them less often. These as a result of the children are getting older.

David no longer babysits. He works and is going to start college next fall. When he's around, he always cooks. David spends more time here than at his parent's home. Sometimes David takes me with him. He likes to drink beer with his friends and his friends like me. One day, I decided I wanted to try beer, so I tipped the bottle over to make a little puddle that l lapped up. I like the taste, and David and his friends thought it was funny. But after a while of doing this a few times, David's friends said, "He's doing it on purpose. Let's show Oscar what beer is really like if you have a little too much of it." So they poured more beer into a bowl. I kept drinking it until I felt woozy. I was not sure what was going on. I was staggering and falling down. David's friends were all laughing at me. "Look at the dog get drunk." Eventually, I threw up, and the next day I had a terrible headache. I never drank beer again. Even the smell of beer makes me feel sick.

A couple blocks from the projects, there is a small variety store. It is owned by an elderly man and his wife, Jack and Sally King. The store is located halfway between the projects and the old house. Marcia, the children, and David all shopped there from both places. Jack and Sally live in a small apartment above the store. They have lived there and have run the store for more than fifty years, maybe even closer to sixty years, long before the projects were built.

Jack's store has a lot of basic foods. He cuts his own cold cuts and grinds his own Hamburg. The store had the largest penny and nickel candy counter in the county. It was always well stocked with the best candy. Jack gave all the children six pieces of penny candy for a nickel or six candy bars for a quarter.

The King's store had a diverse group of customers. Some lived in expensive houses and drove nice cars. Others were welfare families who lived in the projects. Jack knew his customers well and he never forgot someone's name. He would extend credit to his less well-off customers when others would not. Sometimes, customers with overdue bills would send their children in to make a purchase of something for dinner like hotdogs and beans. Jack knew these people were trying to take advantage of him, but he could never let a child go hungry. He knew these people were basically honest and would repay him when they could.

Some of the older teenagers would enter the store as a group. While one or two would try to distract Jack, others would shoplift items from another area of the store. Jack caught on to this rather quickly. In order to combat this, Jack set up a doorbell like button under his counter. When he pushed it, a buzzer would ring up in his apartment. When the buzzer went off, Sally would come halfway down the stairs and sit where she could see every corner of the store. This stopped the shoplifting problem in its track. Jack would threaten to call the police. He never did, but he would ban the person caught from his store for a while. He explained to Sally, "These are not bad children. They just have to be guided in the right direction."

Debbie first took me to Jack's store when I was just a puppy. Often all dressed up in doll's clothes. Debbie said, "Look, Uncle Jack, this is my new puppy, Oscar. I found him in the swamp last winter. He is a lot bigger now."

Jack liked the children to call him Uncle Jack. He and Sally never had children of their own. Debbie got her nickel's worth of penny candy. She was trying to feed me a piece of candy when Jack said,

"Don't give the dog candy. It's not good for him. I have some meat scraps. Give him these instead." I immediately took a liking to Jack, and every time I went there with one of the other children, he always had something for me.

Chapter 9

Fourth of July

Marcia and David go to a lot of places together. They often take me for rides in the car. I love to stick my head out the window with the wind blowing over my nose and the breeze blowing by my ears. It gives me the sensation of flying. Marcia and David like to go to the ocean often. I always run into the surf, even if I know they are going to yell, "Oscar, you are all wet. We will have to wrap you in a blanket or towel." All wrapped up, I enjoy the ride home with my head sticking out of the window.

School is out for the summer. In years past, Susan or Debbie would spend most or part of their summer vacation in New Hampshire with their father and stepmother. This year their father bought a farm with horses, cows, and chickens. He had a big farmhouse with plenty of bedrooms. After sharing a room in the projects, along with the idea of spending time on a farm with separate bedrooms, the girls both decide to go to New Hampshire. Steven refused the offer from his father. Steven and his dad never got along since Steven was young. However, their relationship was getting better as Steven got older.

We are going to spend the Fourth of July weekend at Marcia's brother, Kevin's house. He lived about two hours away. Marcia, David, Steven, and I were driving on Friday the third and coming back Sunday the fifth.

I love to ride in the car with my head sticking out of an open window. They will only open the window enough for me to stick my nose out. I wish they would open it more. It's not like I am going to jump out. When we get to Kevin's, the first thing I can smell is that he's got a cat in here. In the projects, all the cats know where I live. They do not dare cross my property lines. At least if they know what is good for them.

I will let this cat know that I am here now, and if it knows better, it should hide from me while I am here. I start barking loudly to announce myself. All the people yell at me, "Oscar, stop barking."

The cat's name is Satch, short for Satchamo. It's the nickname for Louie Armstrong, a black jazz musician. Satch has other ideas about me. "I am the main cat of this house. I will not let a dog intruder intimidate me in my own home."

I don't see any cats anywhere around me. But unknown to me, the cat is totally black sleeping on top of a black book case. I am thinking the cat must be hiding or outside, so I dose off into a sleep. Suddenly, I awake with this big black monster that landed on my head, swiping at my eyes and nose. I am bleeding from my nose and start barking at the cat.

Well, everyone in the house was sleeping. They all got up and started yelling at me, "Oscar, we told you to leave the cats alone or we will put you outside." The cat disappeared. I was happy just to go back to sleep. After a few hours later, I awoke to see the big black cat standing over me. I dared not bark. I am just looking for a truce. The cat was totally changed. It started purring and licking my nose that was earlier scratched.

The next morning when I awoke for the day, the black cat was hissing at me again. Why is this cat so strange? I wonder. One moment it's about to attack me, the next it's trying to heal me or make me feel better. I must avoid the cat for most of the day.

In the afternoon, we all get into Kevin's van. We are going to a community barbecue, a cookout, with fireworks in the evening. I had never been to any of these type of events, but the people all around appeared to be very excited about the activities that were about to happen.

There were a lot of games, some between parents and children. Like the lawn game of Bacchae Ball, a croquet field is set up, and both children and adults play this. One good thing about this game is that neither the adults nor the children have an advantage. The first competitive game is a softball game played between the policemen and the firemen. The firemen won. Kevin and Steven won the men's three-legged race.

It seemed like everyone brought a grill to cook on. There was all kind of food, including hamburgers, steaks, sausage, and chicken. I am not allowed to eat chicken because of the bones. After everyone was done eating, the firemen dug a big ditch for people to dispose of their coals in. When all the coals were placed in the ditch, it was sprayed with water then buried.

Kevin, Steven, David, and I played with a Frisbee until it was getting dark. Marcia and Kevin's wife put all the leftovers and utensils back into the van. They retrieve some blankets to sit on to watch the fireworks.

I have never experienced fireworks, so I did not know what to expect. *Fizzle, bang, nang,* and the sky was filled with falling pieces of fire. It scared me so badly that I started to shake. That was just the beginning. There were more, a lot more. I could not stop or control my shaking. I stated barking and jumping into the air barking. Marcia told Steven to put me in the van.

Inside the van, I could not see the sky, but the noise just kept on getting more often and louder. I was thinking maybe I should have stayed back at the house with that crazy cat. The end of the fireworks was the worse with many more loud blasts. I was shaking so badly I thought I might die. When it was over, everyone was laughing, joking, and claiming that was the best show they'd ever seen. Back at Kevin's house, I try to avoid the cat at all costs. I have had enough drama with the fireworks. I don't want to deal with that mean black cat again. The next morning we drive back to Marcia's house in the projects.

A day or two go by when I hear Marcia and Steven talking about going to Mrs. King's funeral.

Steven asked, "Jack's wife? How did she die?"

Marcia replied, "She had a heart attack on the Fourth of July."

Immediately, I think that she must have gone to the fireworks. That could give anyone a heart attack. I almost had one.

Susan and Debbie are still in New Hampshire. Steven and his friends don't want me to go along with them. Most of the other project children that I often go with are at summer camp. I decide to visit Jack at his store. When I get there, the store is not open. I bark a couple of times. The sun is warm, and with nothing better to do, I take a nap on the steps in front of the store. This becomes my routine for the next few days. One day, Jack comes out of the store and says, "Oscar, I have seen you coming here the last few days. I know you miss her too, but life must go on. Tomorrow, I will reopen my store. I know you must be lonely too, with the girls in Vermont or New Hampshire. Come on in. I have reordered supplies and I have some meat scraps for you."

Time passes quickly and the summer is going into August and it is still very hot. It is late one afternoon when there is a knock on the door. It is Mrs. Johnson from the old neighborhood. Marcia says, "Mrs. Johnson, what brings you here?" She replies, "Look in this box," as she opens the cover of the box she is holding. Inside the box are four little puppies. The puppies have the same markings as Oscar but the hairstyle of a French poodle. "Your dog and my poodle have made a litter. I can't keep them. My husband is in the service, and we are being relocated to Germany. I must find a home for the mother poodle as well." Debbie is on the phone with Marcia and hears the conversation, "Mother, they sound so cute. Can we keep them?" Marcia replied, "You know we can't. Your uncle can't keep his pets because he's moving, and you told me that you are bringing that thing back from New Hampshire next week."

Mrs. Johnson piped up, "The vet told me that he could find them all a home on a farm in Lancaster PA, but he has a condition. Both dogs must be fixed to avoid any more unwanted litters. I left my dog with him overnight for her procedure. I could take Oscar there when I go to pick her up. He said the procedure for a male is much simpler than a female. Oscar will not have to stay overnight just a couple of hours."

Marcia responded, "Maybe we can go together. Oscar does not like to go to the vet's. I should be with him. We can drop him off and then we can go out for lunch. We can catch up on old times. When are you going to move to Germany? The procedure should only take a few hours, so we can pick up both dogs together. I really should have had Oscar fixed much earlier. I am so sorry that this happened."

Fixed? Fixed? I did not think I was broken, and I'll never have any more pups. At least all my litter will stay together.

Chapter 10

2 Cats 1 Mouse

After returning from the vets, I recall a phone conversation between Marcia and Debbie. "Your Uncle is bringing his pets here and you are moving that thing down from New Hampshire."

Pets? Does Kevin have more than one? All I remember is that mean black cat that pounced on me. What could that thing be that Debbie is bringing home with her? What could it be? It can't be her horse. A horse is too big for the house. I hope it is not a big spider or a snake. I don't like either of those things.

It is Labor Day weekend, when Kevin and his wife arrive on Saturday afternoon. The girls will return from New Hampshire on Monday. Kevin and his wife will stay in the girl's bedroom for the weekend. They bring their suitcase in and bring it upstairs.

Marcia asks, "Did you bring the pets?"

Kevin replies, "Yes, they are in the van. I'll get them now." Kevin soon returns carrying a pet transport box. He opens the box and a totally black cat emerges. I think, "Oh my god, it is that mean cat. It scratched me and made me bleed. Is that what I am going to have to live with?"

Kevin said, "I'll be right back with the other one." He soon returns with another travel box. When he opens it, another totally black cat enters the room. I can't believe my eyes. The cats look exactly alike. They must be twins. How will I tell them apart?

Marcia asks Kevin, "Which one is Satch, and which one is Missy?"

Kevin replies, "Satch is the male. He is very temperamental. If you get him upset, he will try to bite or scratch you. You should be wary of him. Missy is the female. She is very docile. You can pull her tail or throw her in the air and she will only purr. It may take awhile, but you will eventually be able to tell them apart."

The cats look so much alike that I can't tell what gender either one is. I am not going to get that close enough to tell without risking an eye. I will stay away from both of them, at least for now.

Marcia told Kevin, "Tomorrow they have the 4H fair. They will have farm exhibits. Blue-ribbon prizes for pies and pickles. There will also be a horse plow pull and a tractor pull. Picnic baskets are allowed, but grills are not allowed. But of course, they sell food at all the concession stands. We should just plan to buy food there. It will be much easier."

Jan asked, "Will they have fireworks in the evening?"

Marcia answered, "Yes, but we should leave Oscar here. He will still hear them but not be able to see them. My neighbors are away for the weekend, so if he barks, he won't disturb anyone." I think, "Thank god. I have seen enough fireworks to last me a lifetime. After all, I am convinced that it was the fireworks that killed Mrs. King!"

The next day, all the people go to the fair. Suddenly, I know I am alone with the cats. I will try to lay low to avoid the cats. However, the cats are not used to this house, so they are both hiding. As soon as it gets dark, I can hear the explosions from the fireworks. I run up the stairs and hide under Marcia's bed. Suddenly, I realize I am not alone. A black cat nestles next to my face and starts purring. This must be Missy trying to comfort me.

Monday is Labor Day. The girls are returning from New Hampshire. Kevin brings the suitcase and the two empty carriers out to his van.

Marcia asks, "Kevin, you are not leaving now, are you?"

"No, I want to see my nieces before we leave. Jan and I have not seen the girls all summer," Kevin answers. I realize now the cats are here to stay because the transport boxes were empty. I have not seen Satch since he arrived here. That is OK with me. We will have to develop a truce between us.

David knows that Susan and Debbie are returning from New Hampshire, and Kevin and Jan are going to be at Marcia's house. So he had planned a cookout. He marinated steaks and chicken, and made a couple of salads. He plans on starting the charcoals around noon, but he will wait until Susan and Debbie get home before he starts.

The girls arrive home about eleven thirty. Marcia invites her ex-husband and his wife to stay for the cookout. But they refuse because they say they made reservations at a local restaurant that they like.

After the girls bring in their luggage, Debbie retrieves a large box from the car. She removes a large fish tank from the box. The tank contains wood chips, a water bottle, a ladder attached on one side and a wheel. On the top, there is a wire screen with holes about a quarter of an inch wide. The tank also contains a white mouse. When Marcia sees the mouse, she comments, "It's so cute. It's all white with pink eyes and a long pink tail. When you told me on the phone that you were bringing home a mouse, I thought it was one of those grey wild ones. You know, with black eyes and a leathery tail."

Kevin, his wife, and Steven all enter at the same time. Kevin asks, "What is all this commotion about?"

"It's all about my cute new pet. It is a mouse," Debbie replied.

Jan, Kevin's wife, said, "It is so cute, look at the funny way it wiggles his nose. Is it a boy or girl mouse?"

My father told me, "You can't really tell with mice unless you put two together and one has babies, then you can tell." Susan piped in, wanting to be part of the conversation.

Steven inquires, "What does a mouse eat?"

Debbie answers, "It will eat almost anything but meat. The man at the pet store told me I should feed it rabbit pellets because they are all grain. Grain is very healthy for most animals. Cows and horses only eat grain. Did you know that?"

David enters through the back door and announces, "The charcoals are just about ready and I am going to start cooking soon. Who wants chicken and who wants steaks? Oh, hi Mouse. Look I picked some clover for you." He walks over to the cage and puts the clover inside.

Marcia replies, "David, just cooks all of the food and we will decide when we eat. It is better to store cooked meat than raw meat."

I am getting jealous. I use to be her cute pet when I was a puppy. Now I am just her dog. Puppies turn into dogs, but mice are always mice. The girls didn't even greet me when they arrived home. I am feeling a little neglected. I bark twice.

Three people simultaneously shout, "Stop that barking, Oscar."

Debbie said, "Be quiet or you'll scare Mouse." If she thinks that barking scares the mouse, wait until the mouse sees the two cats.

After eating, Kevin and Jan leave. They still have a long ride home. They both are still upset that they had to give up their cats. They had the cats for a few years and the cats were hiding since they got to Marcia's house.

Soon after Kevin and Jan leave, the cats come downstairs. They have been hiding upstairs. They came down only to eat. They had a litter box set up in the bathroom upstairs. Satch notices the mouse right away and jumps up onto the table next to the fish tank. He starts to scratch at the glass like it was not there. The mouse is scared and hides under the wood chips and cotton balls that make up his bed.

Debbie observed this. She grabs Satch by the back of his neck and throws him to the floor yelling, "Satch, you leave my mouse alone or you'll be very sorry."

She got several scratches on her hand and arm in the process. She turns to Marcia crying, "Mother, why did you let this monster of a cat comes here?"

Marcia replies, "If we did not take them, they would have had to put to them to sleep. Where your uncle is moving does not allow pets."

"Well, I hate to see any animal put down, but those cats can't get at my mouse."

David spoke up and said, "Debbie, we will make sure that the house for your mouse is cat proof. They can't get through the glass. All we have to do is make sure the screen on the top is secured. We can get some of those big rubber straps that they use on luggage to secure the top. Meanwhile put something heavy on the top to keep it down."

Debbie replies, "I know if I put my penny jar on top of the screen, no cat can get it off, but thank you, David."

Missy came downstairs and looked at the mouse and completely ignored it. She just went into the kitchen and ate her food. Content after eating, she jumps into the chair where I am. She lies down next to me and stars to purr. I never thought that I would like a cat, but Missy is different.

After a while, I can tell the cats apart. They have a different scent about them. Dogs have a much more intensive sense of smell than a lot of other animals or people. I guess it is because we have a longer nose than most. If that is true, I wonder what an elephant can smell. Satch and I have come to some kind of agreement. He will let me get close enough so I can pick up his scent but no closer.

Mouse still gets all the attention. Every time someone enters the house, they run over to greet him. "Hi, Mouse, how are you?" Mouse always comes out to greet them, even if Mouse is sleeping. David always brings something for Mouse, usually something healthy, but sometimes a piece of cake. David never brings me anything anymore. He used to bring me treats when I was a puppy. My jealousy is becoming more of a problem.

Satch and Mouse have an interesting relationship. Mouse knows that the cat cannot get into his secured home. That does not deter Satch. He always jumps on the table next to the tank. Mouse will come right next to the glass where the cat is at. Satch will jump on to the top where the screen covers the tank. Mouse will climb up the ladder attached to the side of the tank. Then Mouse will walk upside down on the screen and bites Satch where he sits on the screen, sometimes on the tail or the bottom of his feet. It hurts enough so the cat will jump off. Missy always ignores Mouse, her attitude is, "If it doesn't bother me why should I bother it?"

David picks up on my jealousy for Mouse and starts to tease me. Now when he comes over he shouts, "Hi, Oscar, I am here with a mouse in my pocket, but I have many pockets you have to find it."

I go wild jumping all over David, sniffing and scratching at every part of his clothes, looking for the mouse in his pocket. He never has a real mouse. Sometimes, he has a cotton ball that looks like a mouse sticking out of his pocket. But he never has a real mouse. He will yell, "OK, Oscar, that is enough. Stop now!" I always stop then David has a treat for me and says, "Good dog Oscar, you're a good dog."

Mouse on the other hand is not completely defensive. Mouse does not like cats or dogs. It knows that by running on its wheel slowly it makes sounds that people can hear. However, if it runs the wheel faster, it makes a sound only dogs and cats can hear. It is a high frequency sound like a dog whistle. Mouse only knows about the cat that bothers it. So when Mouse get on the wheel to make these painful frequency sounds, Mouse does not realize it affects Oscar and Missy.

When Mouse is making these high frequency sounds, Missy will try to lie over my ears to protect me. When Satch is all over Mouse's cage, if Mouse cannot reach him to bite him, Mouse will get on the wheel and run like the devil is chasing it, making these high frequency sounds.

Chapter 11

Winter

The children have been back to school for a few weeks now. The girls are both in a new school that is too far away for Oscar to go to. They like the school because it is brand-new with better facilities.

I still go to the old elementary school at recess time. Some of the teachers and older children remember me from the time the girls went there. I am getting to know some of the younger children, many of whom live in the projects. The younger children learned my name from the older ones. I really enjoy spending time at the school. On the weekends, if I start to feel jealous of Mouse, I just go out and find one of my friends from school. A lot of these children do not have pets at home. Those children treat me like I am their pet. Many of the children will take me with them to Jack King's store. Jack usually has a special treat for me. He always s says, "Oscar, you watch out for these children, won't you?"

It is Thanksgiving; and Kevin, his wife Jan, and David are over. Marcia has been cooking all day. She cooked vegetables and made a stuffing, along with a twenty-five pound turkey. I have never seen a bird that big. It is almost as big as I am. Of course it has no feathers, but I know it is a bird. I used to chase birds when I was a puppy. I am not sure if that is the collie or the mutt side of me that I got those urges from.

David takes some of the leaves and little stems off the celery that Marcia is putting into the stuffing. He puts them into Mouse's tank.

Mouse goes crazy eating those leaves and stems like there is no tomorrow. After everyone finishes eating, David makes a plate for me and one for each of the cats. The cats each have their own plate. I have my own plate as well. David puts turkey, stuffing, squash, and cranberry jelly in each plate. I like everything except for the squash. I even like the cranberry jelly. The cats only eat the meat. They try the stuffing but don't eat it. David notices this and takes the stuffing from the cat's dishes and put it into mine. I will gladly eat it from my dish. I dare not try to eat anything from the cat's dishes even if they won't eat it.

It is almost Christmas time. Marcia, David, and the girls take me in the car to ride around to look at the decorations. We see houses all covered with colored lights. Santa Clause has the sled and his reindeer. Nativity displays, one with live animals. Everyone gets out except me. I am not allowed out.

After a while, they return with a man carrying a large tree. He ties the tree to the roof of the car. When we get back to the projects, David calls Steven to help him carry the tree into the house. David tells Marcia, "You get the tree stand and fill it with water. I will cut two inches off the bottom to give the tree a fresh cut. Trees need fresh cuts in order to properly absorb the water. The tree should stand for twenty-four hours before we start to decorate it, giving it time to adjust to the indoor temperature and absorb some water."

The next evening, David arrives, and he shouts, "Who wants to decorate a Christmas tree?"

Steven says, "I have been untangling these light strings all day. I get to put the lights on the tree."

Susan replies, "I have been going thru boxes and boxes of ornaments. I think we have too many to put on one tree. Maybe we should get a second tree."

Marcia replied, "No, one tree is more than enough. It is hard enough to clean up after one when the season is over."

Debbie asks, "Can I put the angel on top when the rest of the decorations are done? I know David will have to hold me up, but I want to put the angel on the top."

The tree decorating goes on like clockwork. First, the lights are strung by Steven. Next, Susan put ornaments on. There are many different shapes and size ornaments. Many more than should go on one tree. But Susan makes a good selection. Debbie jumps up and says, "David, pick me up. It is my turn to put the angle on the top."

David replies, "No, it is time for Marcia to put the tinsel on the tree. It must be placed very carefully. Nothing looks as bad as a tree where tinsel looks like it is just tossed on haphazardly."

Marcia is shocked by this. She says, "After all these years of seeing everyone just throwing tinsel at a tree and letting it hang wherever it lands, that can make a tree look like a shaggy dog, I would be most honored to show how tinsel should be placed on a tree. Only one strand at a time."

Steven jumps up and asks, "Can I turn the lights on yet?"

David answers, "Not until your mother finishes with the tinsel, and Debbie places the angle on top."

I am lying down watching all this activity. I am amazed. I have never seen the whole family cooperating like this before. I notice the cats are in another chair and they seem to be observing all this activity as well.

Soon after that, David lifts Debbie to place the angle on top. Then he announces, "Steven, plug in the lights now please!"

Steven plugs in the lights and everyone cheers and claps. Marcia serves hot apple cider with cinnamon stick stirrers. Everyone sit around the tree singing Christmas carols.

Debbie looks out the window and shouts, "Look, everybody, it is snowing. We will get a white Christmas after all."

The cats are intrigued by the ornaments on the tree. Missy likes to hit the balls located on the lower branches of the tree. A couple of them have mirrorlike spots that Missy can see her own image. When she taps these ornaments, her image swings back and forth and rotates. She became so obsessed with this that she can't stop until one of them falls and smashes on the floor. Missy is so scared by the noise and smashing ball that she runs and hides.

There is another ornament that drives Satch crazy. It is a little bird that is battery operated. It sings every half-hour, tweeting like a real bird, and it has a light sensor. So it will only sing when it is light out, keeping it from waking people up when it is dark. Satch thinks about climbing the tree to get to this bird. But he soon realizes that if he gets on top of Mouse's cage, it is just a short leap to the bird .Once on top of the cage, Mouse starts to bite him on his feet and tail. Satch jumps into the tree, almost knocking it over, just as Marcia enters the room. Ornaments are crashing to the floor. Satch has the bird in his mouth. Marcia grabs him and takes the bird ornament from his mouth. Marcia is yelling at the cats as she sweeps up the broken glass from the floor.

Christmas morning, everyone gets gifts. I get rawhide chews, the cats get balls that leak catnip and Mouse gets a little car. Catnip is like a drug for cats; it make them go like they are drunk. The car that Mouse gets is a big plastic car with two little wheels in the back and one big wheel in the front. The one in the front is just like the wheel in the cage. If Mouse runs on the front wheel, the car moves forward. There is a little control adjustment on this wheel so Mouse can turn it left or right. Mouse does not understand the controls yet.

After Christmas, the snow continues to fall. Behind the projects, there is a large field and behind that is a big hill. Everyone calls it Macdonald's hill, but no one knows why since there are no Macdonald's anywhere.

Steven got a pair of skies for Christmas. Susan got a toboggan that is big enough to carry the whole family on. Debbie got a snow saucer. It is winter vacation, and they are all anxious to try them out on Macdonald's hill.

I follow them. It is amazing to see all three playing together. Usually, each one goes their own way. After a few falls, Steven decides he wants to ride with Susan. Debbie wipes out dramatically, going way up in the air and flipping over. Debbie grabs me then jumps on the back of Susan's toboggan just as it is sliding down the hill. This is the first time I ever sled down a hill. I enjoyed it.

Susan declares, "If everyone wants to ride, then everyone must pull it back to the top of the hill. Oscar, it is your turn. You must pull the toboggan up to the top." Debbie attaches the rope to my collar. I am afraid of climbing up the steep hill.

Steve shouts, "Not that way, Oscar. This way is much easier."

I follow him up a much easier path to the top. The empty toboggan on top of the snow has almost no weight at all, and I enjoy pulling it. When we get to the top, Debbie says, "Oscar, try my snow saucer." She placed me in the middle of the saucer and gave it a little push. I am racing down the hill faster than on the toboggan. At first, I am thrilled. Then suddenly, near the bottom of the hill, I hit a bump. I go flying one way, and the saucer goes flying the other way. I landed with a thump and in pain. I will never ride in a saucer again.

I sometimes go to Macdonald's hill by myself. I see some of the other children from the projects that go to the grade school. These children are always happy to play with me. I will ride on a toboggan but only if someone sits behind me.

One Friday in January, it starts snowing really heavy around eleven in the morning. By three in the afternoon, most companies decided to close. Everyone hits the highway at the same time. As a result, a lot of the motorists got stranded on the highway. Many people abandoned their cars and others had to be rescued by snowmobiles. Saturday morning, it is still snowing heavy and the forecast is for the snow to continue. At noon, the governor addresses the state. He declares a state of emergency. Only emergency vehicles and plow trucks will be allowed on the streets after two o'clock.

David says to Marcia, "We should go to the store and get supplies in case were are stuck here for days. We are almost out of beer. We should pick up a couple of cases."

Marcia replies, "David, if you think I am going to try to drive in this storm you must be crazy!"

David answers, "No, we'll take the toboggan and walk to the package store and then we can stop at Jack's store on the way back. I'll call the package store to make sure they are open. Then I will call Jack King and tell him to expect us. I am sure he would rather sell his perishables then let them go bad in the store. We can ask some of the neighbors if they need anything."

Marcia says, "We can take Oscar. He likes to help pull the toboggan. After getting a list of items from a couple of the neighbors, one of them named Dennis wants to join us on our expedition."

I am glad to go with them to the package store. I pull the empty toboggan by myself. It is about one mile from the projects. But once they put four cases of beer on it, I can no longer pull it by myself.

When we get to Jack's store, Jacks says, "Oh, Oscar, I did not know you were coming too. I will make a special treat for you." He grinds up some end pieces of cold cuts and cheese for me. Jack tells Marcia and David, "I want you to take all the bread, eggs, and milk that I have and give them to any neighbor that might use them. Because I will not get delivery of these items before they go bad. There is no charge for these items because I would rather see them eaten then thrown away."

After leaving Jack's store, Dennis says, "I have never been to his store before, but what a nice man to give food away for free."

Marcia replies, "Jack has always tried to take care of the less fortunate people in the neighborhood. He often lets people slide on their bill and will give them food when they can't pay their balance. He is not like many other merchants."

When we get back to the projects, Marcia asks Susan and Debbie to ask other neighbors if they could use bread, eggs, or milk. Be sure to tell the people it is complements of Jack King. It does not take long for everything to be given away.

It took about a week for things to get back to normal. I still go to Macdonald's hill by myself. Marcia's children prefer to go to an ice skating rink. I am not allowed in the rink, so I go to Macdonald's hill instead. I am having fun with the children there, riding down on their toboggans and then pulling the empty ones up the hill. It is starting to get dark when I decide it is time to go home. I am at the bottom of the hill when suddenly, I hear thump followed by feeling pain. I am hit by a speeding sled coming down the hill. I am hit in my rear quarter, and I go flying. I am in extreme pain and I cannot get up.

It is dark outside when Marcia says to David and the children, "It is not like Oscar to stay out after dark."

Suddenly, there is a knock on the door. When Marcia opens the door, there are two small girls standing there. One of them asks, "Are you Oscar's mother?"

Debbie shouts, "Oscar is my dog. Why do you ask?"

The other girl replies, "Oscar was hit by a sled, and he is lying at the bottom of Macdonald's hill. He won't get up."

David says, "Marcia, I'll get the toboggan. You and I should go get him. Steven, you stay here with your sisters." When Marcia and David get to Oscar, they can tell right away that his injury is serious. Debbie meets them halfway back to the house. She is carrying a blanket.

She tells them, "I thought he might be cold."

Marcia says, "Debbie, he is hurt bad. We will have to take him to the animal hospital."

Debbie answers, "I am going with you. I raised him from a puppy."

David tells Marcia, "I will stay with the other children."

The veterinarian tells them, "I gave him a shot for the pain. He definitely has a broken hip. I can't tell if he has internal injuries or not without an MRI. We will have to operate on his hip to put a pin and screws in. If he has internal injuries, that will require another separate emergency surgery. This could become very expensive. You may want to consider the other alternative."

Debbie asks, "Does that mean putting him to sleep? Mommy, we can't put Oscar to sleep. Please?"

Marcia asks the vet, "Can I arrange a payment plan over time?"

The vet said, "Yes, our billing department is known to be quite flexible."

He then says, "Little girl, even if the hip is his only problem, it will take eight to twelve weeks before he can walk again. You will have to put doggie diapers on him every day for most of that time."

Debbie replies, "I don't care. I will take care of Oscar whatever it takes."

Marcia tells the doctor, "Do the MRI and I will make a decision after I know more about his condition. If he has massive internal injuries, it is not fair to him or us either."

Marcia tells Debbie, "I will call the house and tell them what we know so far and that it will be late before we get home."

David tells Marcia, "Steven and I cooked supper and everyone here ate. Have you and Debbie eaten?"

Marcia answered, "No, we will stop at McDonalds on the way home."

The vet returns and says, "Marcia, I have good news. Oscar does not have any internal injuries. We can schedule his hip surgery for tomorrow morning, and you can pick him up any time after four in the afternoon." Marcia approves.

Debbie hugs the doctor and says, "Thank you so much, Doctor."

The next day is Saturday, so there is no school. Debbie has a big coffee can in her bedroom that she has been using as a bank. She wrapped it with a paper that she printed on. "Please help Oscar. Donate to help cover his medical bills. He was hit by a sled and required surgery." Under the text, she places a picture of Oscar. There is still some space under his picture. Debbie tells her family, "I am going to ask Jack King if he will put this in his store. He may help us collect some money to help pay Oscar's hospital bills. A lot of people that go to Jack's store know Oscar."

Later in that day, when she asks Jack if he will allow her to put it in his store, he replies, "Of course, I will, Debbie, but I have a better idea."

Debbie asks, "What is that?"

Jack carefully removes the paper from the can. He writes on the bottom, "Donations can be made at Jack King's store." He writes his address below that. He opens his cash register and removes ten dollars. He hands the paper and money to Debbie and says, "Take these to Staples and have them make color copies. They cost twenty-five cents each, so you can get forty copies. I will give you some thumbtacks. You and your sister put one on every telephone pole and tree in the neighborhood."

Debbie and Susan spend the whole afternoon putting up fliers. When Marcia and Debbie return to the hospital, the doctor tells them, "I want to see Oscar in two weeks for more X-rays. I want to see how Oscar's hip is healing."

Marcia notices all the posters on the poles she said, "I told you it was OK to put the can in Jack's store but nothing like this."

Debbie answered, "It was Jack's idea. He gave me the money to buy the fliers. He also gave me the tacks from his store."

One of the teachers from the elementary school lives in the projects, and he notices one of the fliers and thinks, "This is the dog that comes to play with the children at recess. I wonder if we can do anything to help." He speaks with the principal of the school and shows her one of the fliers. The principal's response was, "Well, we have the annual science fair in the gym on Saturday. We could have a bake sale in the cafeteria at the same time." It is early Monday afternoon when the principal gets on the PA and announces, "We are planning to have a bake sale in the cafeteria on Saturday. The benefits will help pay medical bills for Oscar, the dog who visits us during recess. He has had a bad accident. Anyone that wants to bring in baked items on Saturday morning should bring a note from their parents by Thursday. The note should describe what you plan to bring in for the bake sale."

The response was overwhelming. On Saturday, the school raised $527.50. The teacher who started the fundraising delivered the money to Marcia. Marcia was shocked. She knew nothing about the bake sale at the school. She told the teacher, "I knew nothing about this. How can I ever thank you and the children?"

The teacher replied, "When Oscar can walk again, have someone bring him to the school at recess time. I am sure that is all the thanks the children want." Marcia sent a check to the hospital billing department.

I have been lying on a large pillow in the living room for about two weeks. Debbie changes my doggie diaper every day. I am embarrassed by the diaper, but I cannot walk yet.

When they bring Oscar in for his follow up X-rays, the doctor says, "His hip is healing fine. Debbie, in two weeks you should start exercising his hind legs."

Debbie asks, "How do I do that, Doctor?"

He responds, "Lay him on his back and bend his rear legs at the knees. After a while, he will start to move his rear legs from his hips. But don't hurry or push him. Wait until he starts on his own. In about four weeks, he will start walking gingerly. Again don't rush him, by the end of spring he will be running around like he used to."

Marcia goes to the billing department to inquire about future payments. The person she talks to in the billing department tells her, "An elderly gentleman came in earlier in the day and paid off the balance in full. He told us to send any future bills to him. I think his name was King. Yes, Jack King, that was his name."

Marcia stops at Jack's house after leaving the hospital. Marcia tells Jack, "I don't know what to say, Jack, but thank you!"

Jack replies, "Marcia, when I lost my wife last year, Oscar came every day to visit me, and he kept me company for many days. Seeing him running around will be thanks enough. I am an old man. I do not have much use for money other than to leave it to relatives. Many are just waiting for me to pass on so they can get their hands on my stuff. When I heard when the elementary school had that benefit for Oscar, I realized Oscar is not just your dog. He belongs to everyone in the neighborhood."

Marcia tells Jack, "Oscar is out in the back seat of my car. I think he would like you to come out to visit him." Jack put his coat on and came out to the car.

I was so happy to see Jack. It has been a while, and I can't wait until I can run to his store again.

Debbie starts my therapy. At first it hurts, but every day, it gets a little easier. I will just stay here doing my exercises until I can chase birds and butterflies again. A month has gone by, and I have been getting stronger and stronger. Debbie has been faithfully doing my exercises with me. The teacher that arranged the bake sale is bringing some of the children over to my house to visit me from time to time. I can't wait till I can out got and play with the children again.

I am fortunate that such a caring family adopted me, fed me, cared for me, and taught me how to be a good dog. Most of all, I am fortunate that so many people love me so unconditionally. I am Oscar, and I am a very lucky dog!

The End

About the Author

D. L. Smith was born in a quaint little seaside town north of Portland, Maine. He spoke mostly Canadian French for his first four years. Around the age of five his family moved to a suburb of Boston Massachusetts. Still speaking mostly French, he had a little difficulty in the first grade. By the time he was in High School, he lost his ability to speak French.

The author enjoys traveling. He had the opportunity to live and work in Paris, France for part of 1997 and most of 1998. He had the good fortune of living there when France won the World Cup Soccer Tournament in Paris.

He has visited Austria, Belgium, France, Germany, Holland, Switzerland, Montreal, Quebec, Toronto, and numerous cities in the United States.

The author, now in his early sixties, is the oldest member of a large family.

The author currently resides in Doylestown, Pennsylvania. He often visits New Hope to the North and Philadelphia to the South.

He is an alumnus of North Eastern University, in Boston Massachusetts.